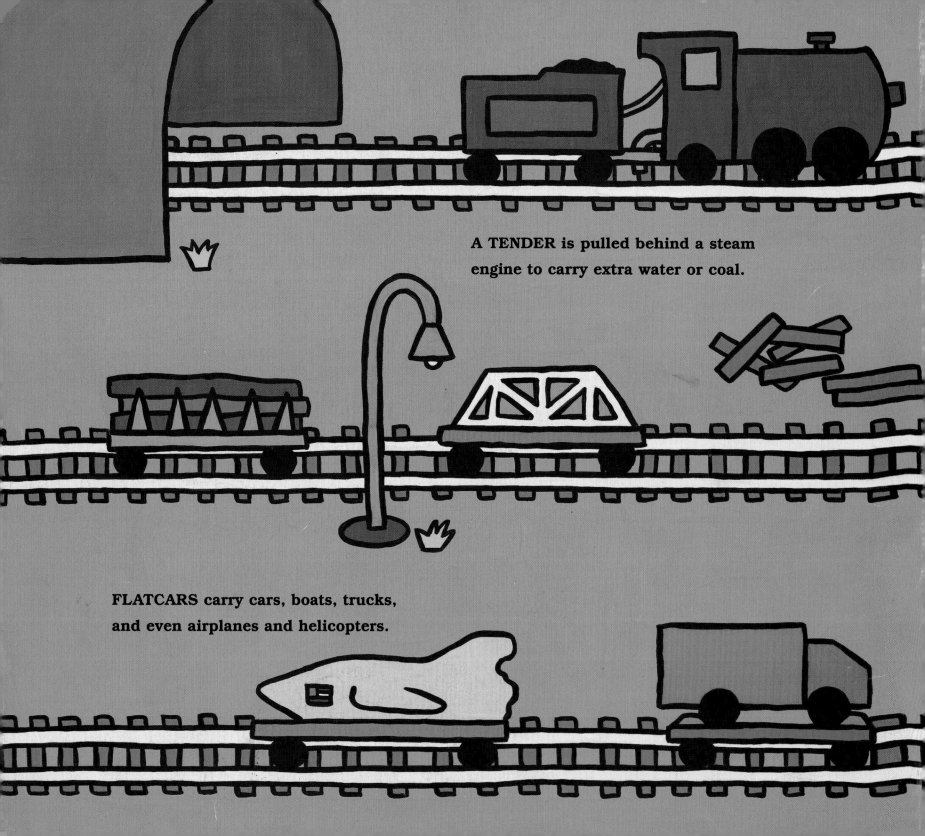

A TENDER is pulled behind a steam
engine to carry extra water or coal.

FLATCARS carry cars, boats, trucks,
and even airplanes and helicopters.

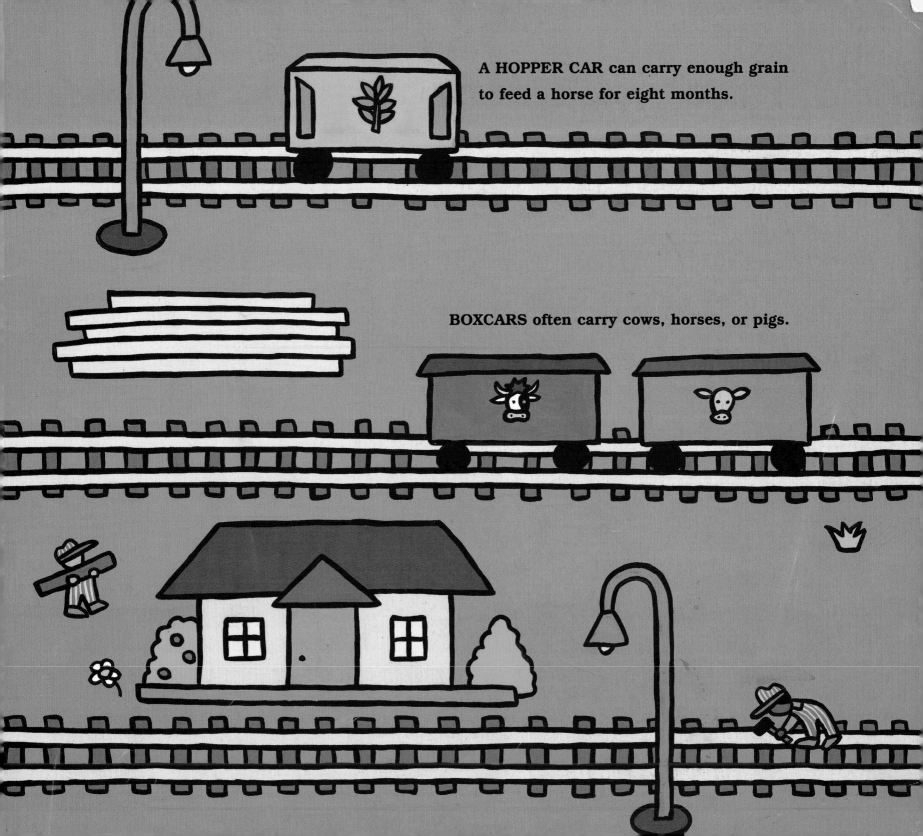

A HOPPER CAR can carry enough grain to feed a horse for eight months.

BOXCARS often carry cows, horses, or pigs.

*To Shari, who loves trains as much as
I do, and to her new child, who will
soon be reading about them*

—P.S.

For Jane

—S.H.

I LOVE TRAINS!

Text copyright © 2001 by Philemon Sturges Illustrations copyright © 2001 by Shari Halpern
Printed in the U.S.A. All rights reserved. www.harperchildrens.com Library of Congress
Cataloging-in-Publication Data Sturges, Philemon. I love trains! / by Philemon Sturges ;
illustrated by Shari Halpern. p. cm. Summary: A boy expresses his love of trains,
describing many kinds of train cars and their special jobs.
ISBN 0-06-028900-7 — ISBN 0-06-028901-5 (lib. bdg.) — ISBN 0-06-443667-5 (pbk.)
[1. Railroads—Trains—Fiction. 2. Stories in rhyme.] I. Halpern, Shari, ill. II. Title.
PZ8.3.S9227 Iae 2001 [E]—dc21 99-86367

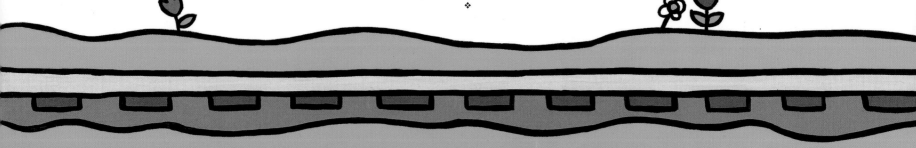

I Love Trains!

BY **Philemon Sturges**

ILLUSTRATED BY **Shari Halpern**

HarperCollins*Publishers*

Trains, trains, trains! I like trains.

I like trains that hoot and roar
as they rumble by my door.

First come engines, big and strong,

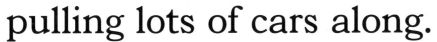

pulling lots of cars along.

Some cars keep things from the rain.

Some cars carry trucks or grain,

or cows

or hogs

or gas

or logs.

Some carry steel; some carry scrap,

or secret stuff that's under wrap.

But the best car's at the end,
and as the train goes round the bend,

I wave.

I'm glad

to see the car that carries Dad.

Trains, trains, trains!
I LOVE trains!

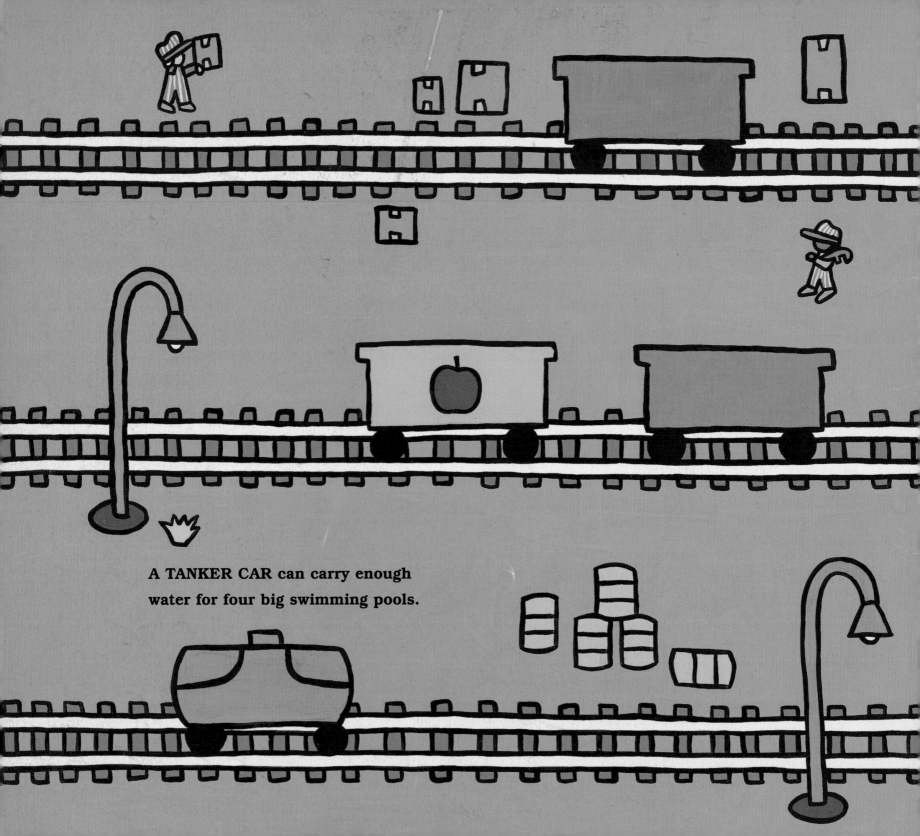

A TANKER CAR can carry enough
water for four big swimming pools.

GONDOLA CARS can carry scrap metal, like old cars and stoves.

The CABOOSE was a place for the train's conductor to sleep.

Trains, Trains, Trains!

A train is passing by! A young boy watches in delight
from his window as it rumbles and roars past. Each of the
cars is carrying something interesting, but his favorite
car is the last one—it carries something extra special!

A cheery, informative book for you~~~~~~~~~~e
trains by the creators of I LOVE TRUCKS!

"A celebration for train lovers.
Toddlers will enjoy making the hoot,
roar, and rumble sounds." —ALA *Booklist*

US $5.99 / $8.99 CAN
ISBN 0-06-443667-5

HarperTrophy®
An Imprint of HarperCollinsPublishers
Ages 3 to 6
Cover art © 2001 by Shari Halpern

50599